To my daughter

I'm Sarah and I love swimming. I love swimming so much my mom says I'm like a fish. But I prefer to be a mermaid instead. That's why I asked my mom to wear my mermaid swimming suit to the pool today.

It was beautiful sunny day and there were many children at the pool. I love making new friends! As I was ready to jump in the pool, I saw a girl wearing another mermaid swimsuit. It was blue and sparkling!

"Wow, your swimsuit is so pretty!"
I said.
"Yours is too," she replied. "But what's that?", she added, pointing to the scar on my chest.
"The doctor fixed my heart because I was sick and now I have a scar," I explained matter-of-factly.

The girl shrugged and jumped in the pool.
I followed her, but I didn't feel like playing in the water anymore. And I didn't like my mermaid swimsuit anymore. I wanted to go back home.

Sarah seemed pensive and upset all day. How can I show her that having a scar is okay? Then, I remembered that an old friend had gone through the same

challenges; her daughter too was born with a heart defect and had needed heart surgery when she was just a baby.

The next day was a sunny day again, but I didn't want to go to the pool.
"How about we invite Suzie and her mother to come swimming with us today?", Mom suggested, with a big smile.
"Who's Suzie? A new friend?" I asked.
"Oh, you'll see. I think both of you will get along well together." And Mom winked.

We arrived at the crowded swimming pool when, all of sudden, Mom waved and shouted, "Hi Rose! Hi Suzie! We're over here!" I didn't want to show my scar with my mermaid swimsuit, so I hid behind Mom's leg.

Suzie and her mother came over. I had never seen Suzie before. She seemed very nice and she was wearing a ballerina swimsuit. And just as I looked closer, I saw a faded line on her chest. Suzie has a scar too! She's just like me!

Suzie wasn't afraid to show her scar. And I wanted to be like her too! She took my hand and we both ran along to play.

We had a lot of fun. We swam, we splashed and we screamed with joy.

"You and I have a lot in common," Suzie laughed.
"It's like we're sisters!" I beamed.

Printed in Great Britain
by Amazon